# IT TAKES
# TWO

# IT TAKES TWO

A novelization by Devra Newberger Speregen
Based on the motion picture

DUALSTAR PUBLICATIONS ™ PARACHUTE PRESS, INC.

## SCHOLASTIC INC.

New York   Toronto   London   Auckland   Sydney

RYSHER ENTERTAINMENT Presents

An ORR & CRUICKSHANK Production In Association With DUALSTAR PRODUCTIONS  KIRSTIE ALLEY  STEVE GUTTENBERG  MARY-KATE and ASHLEY OLSEN  "IT TAKES TWO"

PHILIP BOSCO  JANE SIBBETT  Music By SHERMAN and RAY FOOTE  Co-Producers LAURA FRIEDMAN  ANDY COHEN  Edited By ROGER BONDELLI, A.C.E.  Production Designer EDWARD PISONI

Director of Photography KENNETH D. ZUNDER, A.S.C.  Executive Producers KEITH SAMPLES  MEL EFROS  Written By DEBORAH DEAN DAVIS

Produced By JAMES ORR and JIM CRUICKSHANK  Directed By ANDY TENNANT

RYSHER
ENTERTAINMENT

## DUALSTAR PUBLICATIONS  PARACHUTE PRESS, INC.

Dualstar Publications
c/o 10100 Santa Monica Blvd.
Suite 2200
Los Angeles, CA 90067

Parachute Press, Inc.
156 Fifth Avenue
Suite 325
New York, NY 10010

With special thanks to Robert Thorne, Judi Schwam, and Fran Lebowitz.

Printed in the U.S.A.
First Scholastic printing, December 1995
ISBN:0-590-85310-4
A B C D E F G H I J

# Chapter 1

Amanda Lemmon jammed her baseball cap onto her head and swung it around backward. She pulled at the shoulder of her dress and got ready to swing her bat at the ball.

"Amanda!" Diane Barrows yelled out the window of New York City's East Side Children's Shelter. "Stop! What are you doing? I told you not to play ball in that dress!"

"Why do I have to wear a dress anyway?" Amanda yelled back. "I look stupid."

"You look beautiful," Diane assured her.

Diane was a social worker at the East Side Children's Shelter. She had long brown hair and lovely brown eyes.

Diane helped find families for the children who lived at the shelter. Today she was taking Amanda to meet a family who wanted to adopt her.

Amanda was an orphan. She had no mother or father, and she lived at the East Side Children's Shelter.

Amanda's friend Anthony turned to her. "They're not going to make you live with the Butkis family, are they, Amanda?"

"At least I *got* an interview," Amanda said.

All the kids at the shelter knew about the Butkis family. They'd adopt *anyone*. Even nine-year-olds like Amanda. Most people wanted to adopt only tiny babies.

Amanda's parents died when she was very young. Since then Amanda lived with many different families. But none of them adopted her.

Diane was trying to find the perfect family for Amanda. She'd been trying for two years—ever since Amanda arrived at the shelter. Every month Diane arranged for Amanda to meet a new family who might want to adopt her. But every month something went wrong.

Diane rushed out of the building and hurried through the group of kids waiting to play ball.

"Come on, Amanda," Diane said. "Put down the bat. It's time for your interview."

Amanda groaned. Diane pushed Amanda's blond hair off her shoulders. She stared into Amanda's bright blue eyes.

"Amanda Lemmon, I'd adopt you myself if I could," Diane told her.

"So why don't you?" Amanda asked.

Diane smiled at her. "You deserve a mother *and* a father," she said. "And I'm not married. I want to get married. But only to the right man."

"I know," Amanda said. "A guy who gives you that can't-eat-can't-sleep kind of feeling, right?"

Amanda had heard Diane say that about a million times before.

"Right." Diane smiled. "Now, let's go."

"Aw, Diane, please—" Amanda begged. "Just let me hit the ball one time?"

"All right. You have ten seconds," Diane agreed.

A boy named Frankie got ready to pitch to Amanda. Anthony got ready to catch the ball.

"And Amanda *Butkis* steps up to the plate..." Anthony teased.

"Shut up, Anthony!" Amanda shouted. She glared at him. Anthony gulped nervously.

Frankie pitched the ball. Amanda's bat connected with a *whack*!

The ball flew off the fire escape and bounced back into the street. Amanda ran the bases while

Diane whistled for a taxi.

"Hey, Diane," a boy named Tiny called out. "See if that family wants a boy too. Two orphans for the price of one."

Amanda scowled. "Get your own family, Tiny!"

A taxi pulled up and stopped right over a manhole, which was home base. Amanda ran over to the taxi and slid onto the seat next to Diane.

Frankie rushed over and tagged Amanda through the open window. "She's out!" Frankie called to his friends. "We win!"

"You're a dead man, Frankie!" Amanda yelled back at him as the taxi pulled away.

"Let's just get this interview over with," Diane told Amanda. "Then we'll come back to the shelter. We'll have just enough time to meet the bus for camp."

*Camp*, Amanda thought happily. Now, that was something she always looked forward to!

The taxi pulled up in front of the plain brick house where the Butkis family lived. Amanda took a deep breath. She wondered what might go wrong with *this* interview.

Sometimes the couples she met thought Amanda should be sweeter and more ladylike. And sometimes Amanda thought the couple was just plain weird.

She didn't know what to expect from the Butkises.

Amanda and Diane got out of the cab. Diane turned to Amanda. She held out her hand. "Okay. Let's have the gum."

Amanda leaned over and spit a big wad of bubble gum into Diane's hand.

"Hat," Diane said next.

Amanda took off her baseball cap and handed it to Diane. Diane cleared her throat.

"*Other* gum," Diane ordered. She held out her hand again.

*Busted!* Amanda thought. She leaned over a second time and spit out another piece of gum.

Diane turned toward the brick house. "Okay. Here we go." She put her arm around Amanda's shoulders. Together they marched up the steps to the front door.

Diane rang the doorbell. The door swung open. A man and woman stood in the doorway. A very big man and woman—Fanny and Harry Butkis.

*These people look just plain weird*, thought Amanda.

"Oh, isn't she the most precious thing!" Fanny squealed.

"She's a honey, all right," Harry answered.

Amanda forced herself to smile. She gazed at

Diane. Diane smiled the same polite smile.

With a big sigh, Amanda followed Diane inside.

# Chapter 2

Alyssa Callaway was also nine years old. She had wavy blond hair, blue eyes, and a round face. She looked just like Amanda Lemmon!

"Alyssa! Welcome home, princess!" someone called.

"Vincenzo! I'm so glad to see you!"

Alyssa hurried down a flight of steps that led away from a small airplane. The plane belonged to Alyssa's father, and she was the only passenger on it. She had just flown from her boarding school back to her home in New York City.

Alyssa ran to Vincenzo, and he lifted her in a giant hug. Vincenzo was her father's butler. He had worked for the Callaway family for as long as Alyssa could remember.

"It's great to see you, Vincenzo," Alyssa said. She looked around the airport. "Where's my father?" She frowned in disappointment. "He forgot I was coming home for summer vacation, didn't he?" She pouted.

Alyssa's father was Roger Callaway. He was very rich, and very busy. Roger and Alyssa lived in a big apartment in New York City. Alyssa's mother died when Alyssa was born.

Alyssa went to an expensive private boarding school. She saw her father only in the summer and on school vacations. This was summer vacation, the longest and best vacation of all.

"Daddy *always* promises to pick me up at the airport," Alyssa complained. "And he's always too busy to make it."

"I'm afraid your father had some important business to attend to," Vincenzo explained. "But *I'm* mighty glad to see you."

"Why, thank you, Vincenzo." Alyssa smiled at him. Then her smile faded. "What was my father's excuse this time?" she asked.

"He's at the summer house," Vincenzo replied.

"Which one?" Alyssa asked.

"The one on Lake Minocqua," Vincenzo told her.

Alyssa knew immediately which house

Vincenzo was talking about. "But that house has been closed for years!" Alyssa exclaimed. "Daddy never goes there."

Alyssa knew that her father and mother once lived there. But her father hadn't been back since Alyssa's mother died.

Vincenzo grinned. "Well, he's there now," he said. "In fact, he's putting the finishing touches on your new room."

Alyssa's face lit up. "Oh, Vincenzo, really? I can't wait to see it." She smiled with happiness. "But mostly I can't wait to have my father all to myself," she said. "All summer long."

"Uh, yes...well," Vincenzo stuttered.

Alyssa looked up at Vincenzo. She had a feeling something funny was happening. "Vincenzo, what's going on?" she asked.

"Um, what do you mean?" Vincenzo said.

Vincenzo grinned at her. "I can't tell," he teased. "I've been sworn to secrecy."

"You mean it's a surprise?" Alyssa smiled in delight. "It's a welcome home party! I knew Daddy was up to something!"

Vincenzo looked away. "Now, Alyssa, I didn't say..."

"Oh, Vincenzo, I'm so happy!" Alyssa interrupted. "I never had a surprise party in my whole life."

*How wonderful of Daddy!* she thought. *I suppose now I'll have to forgive him for not meeting me at the airport.*

Alyssa's smile grew even bigger.

*A whole party just for me! How totally, completely splendid!*

# Chapter 3

Amanda Lemmon sat on her bed in the children's shelter. She hugged her knees close to her body. A tear rolled down her cheek.

Diane poked her head into the room. "Hey, slugger. What gives?" she asked Amanda. "The camp bus is waiting downstairs. Everyone is ready to go—except you."

Amanda wiped her face with her sleeve and sniffled. Diane sat down next to her.

"I'm not going to that stupid camp," Amanda declared.

"I don't blame you. Look at this place," Diane said, pointing around the room. "It's a pigsty. It would take you all week just to make your bed."

"Don't joke. I'm serious," Amanda said.

"I know you are. That's why I sent the bus on without us," Diane fibbed.

"You did?" Amanda frowned, as if she didn't believe Diane.

"How much do you want to bet I did?" Diane asked.

"Fifty bucks," Amanda said.

Diane gasped. Fifty dollars was a lot of money!

"Okay, the truth is I didn't send the bus away," Diane admitted. She smiled at Amanda. "But I will if you want me to. And you and I will sit right here until you tell me what's really wrong."

"I don't want to go to the stupid Butkises," Amanda said.

"I was waiting for that one," Diane said.

"If they're the best I can do, it means I'm hopeless," Amanda said. "Nobody *wants* to go to the Butkises—they go because they *have* to." She sighed. "I'm a reject."

Diane wrapped her arm around Amanda. "You are not. It's just that most people want..."

"Babies. I know," Amanda finished Diane's sentence.

Amanda stared out over the city. Below her, car horns honked, people shouted, and buses roared.

"This place is like a dog pound," Amanda said. "And everybody wants a puppy. Not a nine-year-old, grown-up dog." She buried her face in her arms.

"Hey, look at me," Diane told her. "I'm going to find you the best home in the world. And that's a promise."

Amanda sniffled again. "Okay," she finally told Diane. "But you still owe me fifty bucks!"

# Chapter 4

Alyssa Callaway and Vincenzo hurried to the big, fancy limousine waiting for them. Alyssa stared out the window. The limo quickly left New York City behind. Soon they were passing through one little town after another.

Alyssa watched all the people outside. Parents and kids were playing on their front lawns. Girls her age were Rollerblading in parks and shouting with laughter.

In front of one cozy home, a father was teaching his little boy how to fly a kite.

"They're having so much fun," Alyssa murmured.

Everyone seemed so happy. It made her sad.

She couldn't remember the last time she had fun with *her* father. Seeing him on vacations wasn't enough.

*If only I didn't have to go to boarding school,* she thought. *If only we could be together every day.*

Alyssa rested her chin in her hand and sighed. Maybe her father could show her how to fly a kite this summer at the lake house.

She hoped so.

The limousine stopped for a red light.

"What's all the noise?" Alyssa asked.

A yellow school bus filled with children was stopped next to the limo. Alyssa hit the sunroof button. The sunroof slid back, and she jumped up and stared at the bus. Across from her the children on the bus were singing and laughing. Alyssa gaped at them.

"Vincenzo! Look!" she said in delight.

Vincenzo barely glanced up from his newspaper. "Yes, they're children," he said. "I've seen them before."

"They're singing," Alyssa said. She'd never been with a group of kids on a school bus. It looked like fun.

Vincenzo seemed bored. "Is that what that noise is? I thought we'd struck a dog."

The light turned green, and the bus pulled

away. Alyssa plopped down in her seat.

"Where are they going, I wonder?" she asked.

"Summer camp," Vincenzo replied. "That's the bus for poor city kids, orphans, underprivileged children…that sort of thing."

"Orphans?" Alyssa was surprised. She was rich, and those kids were poor. But they were having a great time while Alyssa felt sad. "I don't understand," Alyssa told Vincenzo. "They were so *happy*."

"Yes," Vincenzo muttered, going back to his paper. "Odd, isn't it?"

# Chapter 5

As Amanda Lemmon looked out of the window of the bus, paper airplanes, baseball caps, and shoes soared over her head. Amanda didn't notice. She was too busy watching what was going on outside.

Amanda didn't get to leave the city very often. The small towns she saw seemed new and exciting to her. There were so many normal families doing so many normal things.

She saw families having picnics. She watched a mother and daughter carrying shopping bags from the supermarket and talking happily together.

Amanda saw two girls who looked like sisters

21

skipping hand-in-hand down the sidewalk. They giggled together over some joke.

She saw a little boy perched high on his father's shoulders. The little boy licked at a huge ice cream cone. Amanda watched as the ice cream fell off its cone. *Plop!* It landed right on top of the father's head.

The father roared with laughter.

Amanda laughed too, but she wasn't feeling happy. Deep down, her heart ached to be part of a family of her own.

If only she had a mother to go shopping with. And a father who lifted her onto his shoulders and laughed when her ice cream fell on his head. Or a sister to giggle with.

"We're here!" someone yelled. Outside, a big wooden sign read CAMP CALLAWAY.

Everyone on the bus let out a wild cheer.

"Yes!" Amanda cried.

Camp Callaway was fantastic. She couldn't wait to get there. Last summer she went swimming and rowing and sailing and even horseback riding.

Nighttime at camp was the greatest. They had campfires, sing-alongs, and cabin raids— Amanda's favorite! Last summer her cabin raided one of the boys' cabins and covered it with toilet paper!

The doors opened. Kids spilled out of the bus and raced to the flagpole. A man and a woman waited wearing Camp Callaway T-shirts. The man smiled and waved at all the campers.

"Hi, everyone! My name's Jerry," he told the kids. "And this is my wife, Emily. We're your head counselors."

Emily said, "I'd like to welcome you all here to Camp Callaway. We've got a wonderful week ahead of us!"

Everyone cheered again.

"I see some familiar faces from last year," Jerry went on. "And you can help us—"

Jerry didn't get to finish his sentence. The kids were too excited to listen. They scattered in every direction. Some ran down the trails. Some ran into the woods. And some kids ran to find their cabins.

Amanda raced into the rough wooden cabin where she was staying. All the girls around her were flinging their bags and backpacks onto the empty bunk beds.

"This one's for me!" A tall girl tossed her suitcase onto the top bunk bed next to the window.

She started to climb up. Amanda grabbed her by the belt and pulled her back down.

"Yo, Carmen!" Amanda exclaimed. "You blind, or what? This is my bunk!" She pointed to the ceiling above the bed. Big letters were scratched into the wood. The letters spelled AMANDA LEMMON.

Carmen made a face. "Girl, you need to get a life," she complained. Then she grinned and tossed her suitcase onto another bunk bed.

Amanda grinned and slapped Carmen a high-five. "Girl, camp *is* a life!"

# Chapter 6

Alyssa's limousine pulled into a grand driveway in front of an enormous mansion.

Alyssa jumped out of the limo and stood gazing about. The house was surrounded by smooth, rolling lawns. Beyond the lawns were woods. And beyond the woods were mountains as far as she could see.

"Oh, Vincenzo! It's gorgeous!" she said. "I think this house is going to be my favorite!"

Vincenzo folded his newspaper and tucked it casually under his arm. "I remember many happy years here," he said.

The front door swung open, and a handsome man stepped out.

"Could this be Alyssa Callaway?" he asked, pretending not to recognize her. "Couldn't be! Why, Alyssa's just a little girl. And *you're* a foot taller than she is."

Alyssa giggled. "Oh, Daddy! It's me…honest," Alyssa said.

"Come here, beautiful," Roger Callaway told her.

Alyssa ran into her father's arms. He caught her and spun her around.

"Oh, honey, I really missed you," Roger said. He gave her a big squeeze. "How was school? Did you have a good trip home? I'm sorry I couldn't meet you at the airport."

Alyssa nodded. "That's okay." She grinned up at her father. "I knew it had to be something really important—like a party maybe."

Roger shot a troubled glance at Vincenzo. He set Alyssa gently down on the ground.

"I didn't say a thing," Vincenzo said.

"I figured it out on my own," Alyssa added. "I should have let you surprise me, but I'm too excited."

"You are?" Roger asked.

Alyssa's eyes widened. "It's still on, isn't it?"

"Yes, of course, but—"

Before he could finish, a woman's voice called out from behind him.

"Oh, Roger!" she bellowed. "She's *darling!*"

Alyssa watched a tall blond woman hurrying toward them. Her diamond jewelery glistened in the sunlight. She wore very fancy clothes. Suddenly she smiled, and Alyssa saw two rows of perfectly straight white teeth.

Her father held an arm out for the woman. He grinned down at Alyssa.

"Alyssa, I'd like you to meet a very good friend of mine, Clarice Kensington," he announced.

Alyssa smiled politely. "Hello, Miss Kensington. How do you do?"

Clarice clasped her hands together. "Well! What a perfect little girl," she gushed. "You and I will be great friends," she told Alyssa.

"Are you here for my party?" Alyssa asked.

Clarice chuckled. "*Your* party?" She turned to Roger. "Roger, don't tell me you haven't told her?"

"Told me what?" Alyssa asked.

Roger patted Alyssa's shoulder. "Come inside, honey," he said. "I can't wait for you to see your new room."

"Yes! What a splendid idea!" Clarice said. "I'm sure you two have *lots* to talk about." She winked at Roger.

Roger turned and hurried across the lawn.

27

"C'mon, princess," he called to Alyssa.

Alyssa turned to follow. Before she took a step, she thought she heard Clarice mutter, "He didn't tell her! I can't believe it!"

Alyssa whirled around and stared at Clarice. Clarice gave her a friendly smile.

Alyssa frowned. *Something strange is going on here*, she thought.

Alyssa ran after her father. She caught up with him in the doorway of the most incredible bedroom she had ever seen. She was amazed. It was even better than her bedroom in their New York apartment!

There was a large bed with a ruffled canopy. Toys, books, and stuffed animals filled the shelves.

"Like it?" her father asked. "I tried to make it perfect for you."

"Thank you, Daddy. It *is* perfect. It's the best room I ever had," Alyssa told him happily. She walked over to the window and peered outside.

Roger put his arm around Alyssa's shoulder. "See that place over there?" he asked, pointing into the distance. "Through the trees? That's Camp Callaway. That camp was your mother's idea. I started it right after she died. She had a soft spot for kids without families. She wanted them to have a great place to spend their summer vacations too."

Alyssa's eyes widened. She turned and looked up at her father. "I think I saw those kids on a bus. They were singing. They seemed really happy to go to camp." She smiled at her father. "Mother would have been glad."

"Yes. Um, about your mother—" Roger started to say. He seemed suddenly uncomfortable. He sat on Alyssa's bed and patted a place next to him. "Honey, come sit here next to me. We need to talk."

Alyssa sat down next to her father. Roger cleared his throat.

"Alyssa, a lot has happened while you were away at school," Roger began. "You see, ever since your mother passed away, well, I haven't been able to come up here." Roger stopped and gazed through the window at the camp across the lake.

"But, there comes a time when you have to move on," Roger continued. "And you're getting older and there's only so much a father can do— uh—without help."

Alyssa scrunched up her nose. Her father wasn't making much sense. "We have Vincenzo to help," she pointed out.

Roger fingered his shirt collar. "That we do,"

he replied uncomfortably. "But a little girl needs a—"

"Mr. Callaway!"

Vincenzo's voice boomed through the house. "Boss! It's your office on the phone! They need to talk to you right away!"

Roger sighed. "I'm sorry, honey. I have to take this call. We'll talk later, okay?" He gave Alyssa a big hug.

Alyssa nodded. When her father was gone, she went back to the window and stared through the trees at Camp Callaway.

She imagined camp was a fun place where children laughed and sang all day. Every summer of her life she'd gone away with her father. They usually went places where there weren't many children. Not that those summers were *bad* or anything. Just a little boring.

*Just once, I'd like to go to camp*, Alyssa thought. *But I guess it will never happen.*

# Chapter 7

Amanda stood near the camp flagpole and stared through the trees. She could see the huge Callaway mansion across the lake.

"Check it out!" Frankie cried. Carmen, Anthony, and Tiny rushed over. Frankie pointed where Amanda was looking.

"Whoa! That place looks like a palace!" he announced.

Amanda rolled her eyes. "That's no palace, stupid," she said. "That's the Callaway house. It's a big, fancy mansion."

"Nobody's lived there for years. It's haunted!" Anthony told the others.

Amanda made a face. "It is not."

Tiny balanced on a large boulder. "Is too!" he insisted. "Every full moon old lady Callaway's ghost crosses the lake." He paused. "And she eats one of the campers!"

"She does not!" Amanda insisted.

Carmen put her hands on her hips. "You ever been over there?" she asked Amanda.

Amanda shook her head. "No," she replied. "But I'm not scared." She straightened up and tucked her brown T-shirt into her denim overalls.

"If you're so sure it isn't haunted, then why don't you go over there and ring the doorbell?" Frankie dared Amanda.

The kids exchanged looks of disbelief. "You think I'm scared?" Amanda asked.

"Five bucks says you're chicken," Frankie said.

"Cough it up!" Amanda said. "Show me your money."

The kids reached into their pockets for their money.

Amanda held out her palm. *This was going to be easy!*

Alyssa stood by the tall window in the den. She peered through a telescope at Camp Callaway. She saw several wooden cabins. That must be where the orphans slept.

She aimed the telescope at the grassy area near

the flagpole. A bunch of kids were playing a game. It looked like a lot of fun. They wore shorts or overalls and T-shirts. They didn't care if their clothes got torn or dirty.

A pretty woman with long, dark hair played with the kids. She leapt and jumped and laughed as much as they did. Alyssa never saw an adult play with children that way before.

*Thunk!*

A noise sounded outside in the hall. Someone was coming into the den.

Alyssa quickly ducked behind the drapes. A moment later, Clarice breezed into the room. She was followed by a team of people dressed in white uniforms.

"Now, we'll have food and drinks in here. And also on the patio," Clarice ordered.

Clarice gazed around the huge room. A look of disgust crossed her face. "Ugh, how I *hate* this room! Roger's first wife had no taste at all. I can't wait to sell this house."

Alyssa gasped. *Sell it?*

She pushed the heavy drapes aside and stepped into the room.

Clarice saw her and began to sputter. "Oh, uh, well, *hello,* munchkin!" she said with a big fake smile.

Alyssa felt a lump in her throat the size of a

tennis ball. She glared at Clarice and stomped into the hall. She took a deep breath and screamed at the top of her lungs.

*"Daaaaaaddddddyyyyy!"*

Doors flew open everywhere. Everyone in the house came running. Roger appeared at the top of the stairs. He saw Alyssa screaming and ran to her.

"Sweetheart! Are you all right?" he asked breathlessly.

"No! I'm not!" Alyssa fumed.

"What's happened?" her father asked.

Clarice appeared in the hall with a tight smile on her face. "Alyssa was hiding in the den. She heard something I said," Clarice said calmly.

Alyssa pointed a finger at Clarice. "She hates this house!" she blurted out.

"Oh, no. You've got it all wrong, dear," Clarice insisted. "I simply said we might fix it up some-day," she told Roger. "That is, if you'll let me."

Roger looked helplessly at Vincenzo. He knelt down at his daughter's side. "Well, I guess there's no easy way to say this," he began. Roger's fore-head crinkled in concern. "Alyssa honey, Clarice and I are getting married next month. She's going to be your new mother. Isn't that great? The big party tonight is really for Clarice and me. It's our engagement party."

Alyssa gasped. "No!" she said. She stared at her father. "Noooo!" she shrieked. Her voice rose higher and higher.

Roger and Clarice and all the workers stared at Alyssa. So Alyssa did what she always did at times like these.

She fainted.

That is, she pretended to faint. Her father leapt forward and caught her before she hit the floor. He held Alyssa in his arms and glanced at Clarice. "She does this sometimes," he explained.

"*And* she gets away with it," Clarice complained. "Put her down, Roger. Right now. Little tantrums mustn't be rewarded."

Roger blinked in surprise.

"*Now*, Roger," Clarice repeated. "Trust me. I know what's best for her."

Roger sighed and bent to place Alyssa on the floor.

Clarice clapped her hands loudly. "Okay! Everybody back to work!" she ordered. She pulled Roger out of the hall.

Alyssa wondered what was going on. *Why was Daddy listening to that terrible woman?* she wondered. Usually, he held her in his arms and promised everything would be okay.

Alyssa sat up and opened her eyes. Everyone

was gone, except for Vincenzo. Alyssa felt embarrassed.

Vincenzo brushed her hair off her shoulders. He lifted her chin gently with his finger. "You look like someone who could use some milk and cookies," he said.

# Chapter 8

At that same moment Amanda was looking up at the Callaway mansion. Anthony, Tiny, and Carmen were with her. They crept along the side of the huge house.

"Wait! I think I saw something!" Tiny whispered loudly.

"Me too!" Carmen said.

Amanda waved her hands above his head. "Whoooo! Maybe it's Casper the Ghost!" she teased.

Amanda gazed at the front door and took a deep breath. The place *did* look deserted.

*Good thing I don't believe in ghosts*, she thought.

"It doesn't look *too* haunted," Anthony said.

"That's what they *want* you to think," Tiny said.

Amanda gathered up her courage. While her friends hid behind a cluster of trees, Amanda sprinted across the lawn and ducked behind a tree. She licked her lips. Then she raced toward the front door.

Alyssa found Vincenzo outside on the terrace. She was dressed in the kind of clothes the orphans at Camp Callaway were wearing—overalls and a brown T-shirt.

"I already lost my mother," Alyssa told Vincenzo. "And now I've lost my father as well," she told him. "I have no family. I am an orphan. And I'm running away. Please, try not to worry, Vincenzo. You're my only friend."

She took a deep breath and walked across the porch. She hurried away from the big house. She left by the back yard. She didn't see Amanda, who was at the front of the house.

Just then, Amanda reached the front door of the mansion. She pushed her finger against the doorbell. Hard.

*Brringgg!*

*All right!* Amanda thought. She just made five bucks!

Then something amazing happened. The front door opened. A man in a suit stared down at her denim overalls and brown T-shirt.

"Well, if it isn't the little orphan girl," he joked. "So you decided to stay home after all." He reached out and gave Amanda a big hug. Then he pulled her inside and closed the door.

Amanda gulped. "Look, I didn't mean anything. Ringing your bell was a joke. I was just kidding around, honest."

She looked around the inside of the house.

*Holy Toledo!* she thought. *Get a load of this place!*

Maybe it really *was* a palace! It was definitely the most amazing house Amanda had ever seen.

"Guess you think I'm pretty stupid," Amanda said to Vincenzo. She chewed her gum and cracked a bubble.

"Nonsense," Vincenzo said. "You were just upset." He turned Amanda toward the large staircase. "Well, the joke's over, Alyssa. Let's get you ready for the big party."

*Huh? What party?* Amanda wondered. *And why did this guy just call me Alyssa?*

"Your dress is in your room, on the bed," Vincenzo told her. "The party starts at five."

*What party?* Amanda wondered. *What is going on?*

She frowned at Vincenzo. "A dress for me? You've got to be kidding," she told him. "I never wear dresses."

She glanced up at the stairs. "I have to go now—" she began to say. But she stopped short.

Amanda was really curious. She just had to take a quick look around upstairs. She climbed the stairs to the second floor.

Even the hallway was incredible. She had never seen a place so fancy in her entire life. *This is amazing!* she thought. *I wonder whose house this is anyway?*

She turned a corner, and her jaw dropped open.

In front of her was a big painting. The painting showed a young girl. Only...only the girl in the painting looked exactly like Amanda!

"It's...it's *me*!" she gasped.

She stared at the picture in horror.

How did the painting get there? Her hands began to shake.

"This place really *is* haunted!" Amanda cried.

Just then Clarice stepped into the hall. She wore a long, flowing white robe. Her face was covered with white cream.

Amanda took one look at her and screamed.

"*Eeeaah!* It's old lady Callaway's ghost!"

Clarice gave her an evil grin. "You can run, princess, but you can't hide," she muttered.

Amanda *did* run. With her heart pounding, she

flew down the stairs two at a time. She was out the door in a flash.

# Chapter 9

Alyssa made her way through the woods to Camp Callaway. After every few steps she stopped to glance back at her house.

*Why isn't anyone coming for me?* she wondered.

A woman's voice startled her. "There you are!"

Alyssa whirled around. *It's her!* she thought. *The nice woman from camp!*

"I've been looking all over for you," Diane said.

"You have?" Alyssa asked.

"Sure," Diane replied. "Let's go, slugger," she told Alyssa. "The kids are playing touch football. You're missing out on all the fun."

Alyssa didn't know how to play. But she'd probably have a good time trying.

Diane held out her hand. Alyssa gazed into her eyes. They were the kindest eyes she'd ever seen. She took Diane's hand.

Alyssa gave Diane a small smile. "Okay," Alyssa told her.

Diane led Alyssa to the football field. Some of the kids cheered when they saw Alyssa.

"Uh, hi, everyone," Alyssa said.

Diane divided the kids into two teams, red and blue. She handed Alyssa a belt of red nylon flags and pushed her into the red team's huddle.

Alyssa swallowed nervously. She didn't have the slightest idea what to do.

"Okay, everybody to the left," the red team captain ordered. "Block for Amanda. On four. Ready? Break!"

"Which one's Amanda?" Alyssa asked in confusion.

"Ha-ha," the red team captain said. "Funny."

The quarterback tossed her the ball. Alyssa caught it. *Hey! I caught the football!* she thought. *I'm good at this!*

She glanced up, feeling proud of herself.

A thundering herd of kids was running right toward her. Alyssa turned and sprinted in the opposite direction, screaming.

"You're going the wrong way, Amanda!" the red-team kids called after her.

But Alyssa kept going. She ran off the field and headed straight for the woods.

Amanda flew away from the mansion. She ran toward the woods, trying to get far away from Clarice.

Amanda looked over her shoulder as she ran. *Good! That scary lady wasn't following her!*

Alyssa looked over her shoulder as *she* ran. *Good! The herd of kids wasn't following her!*

Alyssa raced into the woods from one direction. Amanda raced into the woods from the *other* direction.

*Wham! Bang! Crash!*

Amanda and Alyssa plowed right into each other.

They knocked each other down.

The girls both got up on their hands and knees and crawled closer for a better look.

"Ahhh!" they both cried out at the same time.

"Do you see what I see?" Amanda asked.

Alyssa gulped. "I don't know what *you* see, but what I see is...*me!*" she exclaimed.

"I see me too," Amanda said.

"Does that mean there's two of *you*? Or two of *me*?" Alyssa asked.

The girls stood up.

"Wait a second!" Amanda said suddenly. "*You* live in the Callaway house!"

"And *you're* that girl from camp!" Alyssa said.

"They thought *I* was you!" the girls said at the same time.

Both girls stopped to catch their breath.

"What were you doing at my house?" Alyssa asked.

Amanda pointed to the camp. "I made a bet with some of the kids," she explained. "They think your house is haunted. So I bet them I wasn't scared to ring the doorbell. Who's the guy in the penguin suit?"

"Penguin suit?" Alyssa asked. Then she realized Amanda thought Vincenzo's dark suit and white shirt made him look like a penguin.

Alyssa giggled. "That's Vincenzo. He's our butler. Who's the woman with the long, dark hair?"

"That's Diane," Amanda told her. "We're buddies." She stood up and brushed dirt off her shorts. "What were you doing over at camp?"

Alyssa's face turned red. "I wanted to see what it's like to be an orphan," she admitted.

Amanda's eyes widened. "Why?" she asked.

"Because it looked like fun," Alyssa answered.

Amanda stared at her. "Being an orphan?

What's the matter with you?"

The girls stared at each other. "Don't you find this odd?" Alyssa asked. "I mean, we look exactly alike."

Amanda nodded. "Somebody told me that everybody's got a double someplace," she said. "You must be mine."

"Are you a real orphan?" Alyssa asked.

"Yup," Amanda said. "Three days old, I got dumped. Been kicked around ever since. What's your story?"

"My mother died when I was born," Alyssa explained. "It's been me and my father ever since." She made a face. "Until today, that is."

Amanda raised her eyebrows. "What do you mean?"

"Tonight's his engagement party," Alyssa explained. "He's getting married. To a terrible woman!"

Amanda winced. "Not that scary blond lady?"

"That's her!" Alyssa exclaimed. "Clarice Kensington."

"You should get rid of her," Amanda said.

"Any suggestions?" Alyssa asked.

Amanda grinned. "I could think of a few ways." She glanced toward camp. "But I should get going now," she said. "It was really nice meeting ya," Amanda told Alyssa.

Alyssa turned toward the mansion. "Yes. I suppose this is good-bye."

"Hey, wait!" Amanda pointed to Alyssa's waist. She was still wearing the red team's flag belt. "The belt."

Alyssa untied the belt and handed it to Amanda.

"Hang on a sec," Amanda said. "This engagement party—you really don't want to go?"

Alyssa stuck out her tongue. "I'd rather eat dirt."

Amanda rubbed her hands together. "Then today's your lucky day!" she said with a grin. "These are the four words that made me the most popular kid at the East Side Children's Shelter." Amanda paused. "I have a plan!"

Alyssa shook her head in confusion. "A plan?"

"Sure! You be me, and I'll be you," Amanda said. "One night only. Tomorrow at noon we switch back. Whaddayasay?"

"Sounds great!" Alyssa grabbed the flag belt and tied it around her waist again. "Meet you at the stables—tomorrow, at noon!" she said. She was already running back to the camp. "Bye, *Alyssa*!"

Amanda waved. "Catch you later, *Amanda*!"

# Chapter 10

Amanda twirled in front of the mirror in Alyssa's bedroom. She'd never worn anything like this before. She'd never even *seen* a dress so pretty. Actually, Vincenzo didn't call it a dress. He called it a gown.

Amanda stared at herself a while longer. Then Vincenzo came to take her to the party.

Music floated up the stairs. Amanda and Vincenzo walked toward the sound. They stopped at the top of the stairs. Everyone in the hall stopped talking. They were all looking straight at Amanda.

"What's everybody staring at?" she whispered to Vincenzo.

Amanda Lemmon is an orphan. Her biggest
wish is to have a family of her own.

Alyssa Callaway is a rich girl. She has everything in the world—except friends.

Alyssa's biggest wish is to have someone to play with.

Bad news for Amanda! The Butkis family is about to adopt her—and everybody knows Mr. and Mrs. Butkis are really, really weird.

Alyssa receives terrible news too. Her father is about to marry Clarice—a woman who hates kids!

Amanda and
Alyssa have
one totally
amazing thing
in common…

…they look
exactly alike!

When the girls meet, they come up with a great idea: "Let's trade places!"

Amanda becomes a princess! She has never worn such a beautiful dress!

And Alyssa becomes an orphan! She gets to go to camp with other kids. Cool!…

…Until she is adopted by the Butkises, who own a junkyard!

Meanwhile,
Amanda works
on a plan to
rescue Alyssa.

Alyssa is saved—way to go, Amanda!

"You, silly," he replied.

A handsome man waited at the bottom of the stairs. "Alyssa Callaway, you're as pretty as a picture!" he called out.

Amanda had no idea who this man was.

"Aren't you going to answer your father?" Vincenzo whispered.

Amanda tried not to gasp out loud. That guy was Alyssa's dad? *Wow!*

"Uh…hi, Daddy," she replied. She'd never called anyone "Daddy" before. It felt pretty great.

Roger climbed the stairs and led Amanda down the rest of the way. They walked into the party together. Roger introduced Amanda to several guests. Then he was called away.

A waiter approached her. "*Escargot,* miss?" he asked. He held out a tray of delicious-looking round snacks.

"Why thank you waiter-person. I mean, I'd adore one," Amanda replied. She popped a snack into her mouth. "Ugh! This tastes like a balloon!" she said.

"It's a snail, miss," the waiter told her.

*Did he say snail?* Amanda spat the food right back onto the tray. "All this money, and these people eat slugs?"

Amanda made a face. *Maybe I can find myself*

*a chili dog in the kitchen.*

At that same moment, the kids at Camp Callaway were getting ready to eat dinner in the mess hall. Alyssa's mouth hung open in disbelief. Two hundred kids were banging their silverware on the tables. "Food!" they screamed. "Bring on the food!"

The noise was deafening.

Alyssa timidly lifted her own fork and knife. She tapped them slowly on the table.

"Hey! This is fun!" she said. She banged as hard as she could. "Food! Bring on the food!" she screamed.

The kitchen doors opened, and everyone cheered as the waiters hurried in. The waiters were really campers. They balanced huge trays of food. Alyssa couldn't wait to eat. She was starving!

A waiter spooned some bright orange glop onto her hamburger bun. The kids around her dug in. Their faces were soon covered with orange goo. Alyssa's upper lip curled in disgust.

"Amanda, what's with you?" Diane asked. "I thought sloppy joes were your favorite."

Alyssa swallowed hard. "Oh, sure. Right. Of course they are," she replied. "I'm, uh, just savoring the aroma."

Diane shot her a strange look. "Huh?"

Alyssa picked up the food. She forced herself to take a taste. "Wow!" she said in surprise. "This is delicious!"

A few bites later her face was covered in orange goo too!

Amanda looked up and found herself face-to-face with Clarice.

"Alyssa sweetheart, I've been promising everyone that you'll play for us," Clarice said.

*Cool! They want me to play a game,* Amanda thought. "Of course, I'd be delighted. What did you have in mind? Checkers? Dodgeball?" she asked Clarice.

Clarice cleared her throat. "Ladies and gentlemen," she said loudly. "Before we all sit down to dinner, Alyssa, my future stepdaughter, whom I absolutely *adore*, has agreed to play for us. This piece won her first prize at the Windsor Academy Youth Recital this past spring."

*Huh?*

Everyone in the large room applauded and smiled at Amanda. "This way, dear," Clarice said. She pointed Amanda toward a huge piano.

Amanda gulped. "Oh boy, oh boy, oh boy," she muttered under her breath. She bent close to Clarice. "Hold it—time out. I can't play the piano. No way, José. Sorry!"

Clarice bent down next to her. "But I told everyone that you would."

"Well then do me a grand favor and *untell* them," Amanda said.

Clarice leaned over. "Listen, if you embarrass me, I'll make sure you never play *anything, ever again*. Have I made myself clear?" she whispered through gritted teeth.

Amanda stared at Clarice. Alyssa was right. This lady was terrible!

*Fine, lady!* Amanda thought. *But don't say I didn't warn you!*

Amanda marched up to the piano. She plopped onto the bench. She turned to the roomful of guests.

"Ladies and gentlemen," she said, "I'd like to play you a song I wrote for my new mom. It goes a little something like this."

Clarice beamed at her with her big phony smile. Amanda beamed right back. She cracked her knuckles and began to bang on every single key on the piano. She hit the black keys extra hard. The noise was awful!

When she finally stopped, there was dead silence. She turned to Clarice and smiled sweetly. Clarice looked as if she were about to explode.

# Chapter 11

At Camp Callaway, Alyssa gazed happily into a roaring campfire. They just finished roasting delicious marshmallows. Now everyone was playing charades, girls against boys.

Diane gathered the girls' team around her. "Okay," she whispered. "The boys are eight seconds ahead of us." She turned to Alyssa. "Amanda, you're on."

Alyssa stared up at her, wide-eyed. "Me?"

Diane patted her on the back. "You're the best, baby. Show 'em what you got!"

Alyssa stood up. The girls' team cheered. Alyssa never played charades before. She reached inside a big black hat. Her hands shook as she drew out a slip of paper.

Jerry held a stopwatch in front of her face. Alyssa's heart thumped wildly. Everyone was watching her.

Alyssa grinned weakly. She opened the paper and read the clue she would have to act out. It was a song: "London Bridge is Falling Down." Alyssa stared at the words.

Jerry clicked the stopwatch. "Ready, *go*!"

Everyone on the girls' team held their breath. They were waiting for Alyssa to start.

Alyssa gulped. Her mouth dropped open in fear.

"Song!" Carmen shouted. She grinned.

Alyssa took a deep breath. There was only one thing to do.

She fainted.

"'London Bridge is Falling Down'!" Carmen shrieked.

Alyssa bolted up in surprise. "That's it!" she cried.

"We won!" Carmen screamed. The girls crowded around Alyssa and cheered just for her.

Amanda was bouncing high on Alyssa's squishy bed. It was the thickest, most comfortable bed Amanda had ever seen. And it was in the fanciest bedroom Amanda had ever seen.

Toys and books were heaped everywhere. The closet was crammed with fancy clothes.

Someone knocked at the bedroom door. Amanda scampered under the covers.

"Come in," she called.

Roger entered. He sat on the bed. "Mind if we talk?" he asked.

"Whatever about?" Amanda asked him.

"Clarice. I just want you to give her a chance," he said softly. "I mean, after all, wouldn't it be nice to have a mother?"

Amanda figured this was her big chance to help Alyssa. She cleared her throat. "If you ask me, Clarice is a big phony-baloney!" she announced.

Roger stared at her in shock. "I don't remember you being this outspoken, Alyssa. I think you're being a little hard on her, don't you? The person you're really angry at is me."

Amanda's eyes widened. "You? What did you do?"

Roger smiled. "Well, we could spend more time together," he said. "Clarice is going back to the city tomorrow. She has lots to do before the wedding. So while she's gone, you and I are going to spend some time together. We'll get to know each other again. Deal?"

"Deal," Amanda said. She grinned at Roger

and then yawned a big yawn.

Roger kissed her on the head. "Go to sleep," he told her.

"Hey," Amanda whispered.

"What, princess?" Roger asked.

Amanda sighed. "I like having a father," she said happily.

Roger smiled. "Well, I like having a daughter."


Alyssa was also snuggling into bed. She was in Amanda's bunk at camp. She yawned and stretched. And felt something incredibly slimy pounce on her.

"Aaaaahhhhh!" Alyssa screamed and threw back the covers. A huge bullfrog sat right on her chest.

"Ha-ha! Got you, Amanda!" Anthony shouted from outside the cabin.

He and some other boys ran away, laughing.

Diane rushed into the cabin. "What's going on?" she asked. "Amanda, are you okay?"

"I'm not sure," Alyssa said.

"Come with me," Diane said. She brought Alyssa into her own cabin. Alyssa told Diane what happened while Diane brushed and braided Alyssa's hair.

"Too bad that frog got away," Diane said. "I could have kissed it. Who knows? It might have turned into my Prince Charming."

Alyssa giggled. "You'd *kiss* a frog?"

"How else am I supposed to find a guy?" Diane asked.

Diane reached out and tickled Alyssa until she squealed with laughter.

"You remind me of someone," Alyssa told Diane when she stopped laughing.

"Who?" Diane asked.

"Someone I've never met," Alyssa answered. "But sometimes when I dream, I think I see her."

"You're acting awful strange today, kiddo. Must be all this fresh air." Diane grinned at her. "You're usually such a tough guy."

"Don't tell anyone, okay?" Alyssa asked.

"Okay," Diane agreed.

Alyssa grinned happily at her. Now she and Diane were pals too.

# Chapter 12

Amanda woke up bright and early the next morning. She yawned and then jumped out of bed. She started to get dressed. After all, she had only a few hours left to live like a rich girl. And she was going to enjoy them before she and Alyssa had to switch places again at noon.

After breakfast Amanda stood next to Roger on the circular driveway. They watched as Clarice got ready to go back to the city. Amanda chewed a wad of bubble gum.

Clarice was barking orders at everyone. Finally, she hugged Roger good-bye and headed for the limo.

"What about a hug for me?" Amanda asked.

"Well, uh…sure," Clarice said in shock. She leaned close and hugged Amanda. Amanda slipped the wad of bubble gum out of her mouth and stuck it in her hand. She threw her arms around Clarice and gave her an extra-big, extra-long hug.

"Bye, Clarice!" she said sweetly. "I'm going to miss you so much!"

Clarice stared at her in surprise. "Oh, me too, dear." She shrugged and climbed in the limo.

Amanda giggled. A big pink wad of gum was stuck to the back of Clarice's head.

Amanda spent the rest of the morning floating in the huge swimming pool. She felt like a real princess. Especially when Vincenzo brought her a soda on a silver tray.

*Not bad. Not bad at all*, she thought.

After swimming, Roger drove her into town for ice cream. He put down the top on his convertible, and the wind blew through Amanda's hair. She put her hands behind her head and sighed happily.

They ate their ice cream sitting on the hood of the car.

*So this is what it's like to have a dad*, Amanda thought. She was having so much fun, she almost forgot about switching places with Alyssa. Then the big clock nearby chimed twelve.

It was noon. Time to turn into a pumpkin again.

At Camp Callaway, Alyssa was having the time of her life. It was great pretending to be Amanda Lemmon. Nobody suspected a thing.

Alyssa spent the morning splashing in the lake. She swam with the other kids and played water games. Diane even brought her out on the lake and taught her how to fish.

"We can't stay long," Diane told her. "We have to be back at camp at noon."

Alyssa nodded and snuggled up close to Diane. Diane put her arm around Alyssa's shoulders. Alyssa closed her eyes. For a split second she pretended Diane was her mother.

And boy, did that split second feel great.

A little after noon Alyssa and Amanda met at the stables. "How was the party?" Alyssa asked.

Amanda grinned. "Great. The good news is…Clarice is gone."

"You did it!" Alyssa cried.

"Well, the bad news is, she'll be back in a week," Amanda finished.

"Oh, you didn't get rid of her," Alyssa said.

Amanda sat down and sighed. "So what's a cool guy like your dad doing with a creep like Clarice anyway?" she asked Alyssa.

Alyssa sighed too. "I don't know. It's too bad he didn't meet Diane first. Now *she's* awesome."

Amanda nodded. "Yeah. They'd be perfect for each other."

Slowly, the girls turned and stared at each other.

"You're not thinking what I hope you're not thinking, are you?" Alyssa asked.

"Want to bet?" Amanda nodded eagerly.

"What if they *did* meet?" Alyssa asked. "Daddy would see how wonderful Diane is—"

"And fall *out* of love with Clarice and *into* love with Diane!" Amanda finished.

"But he's getting married next month," Alyssa pointed out.

"So? All they have to do is meet!" Amanda said. "They'll fall in love for sure!"

The girls exchanged gleeful looks.

"We could be sisters!" they said together.

Amanda jumped up and began to pace the dock, back and forth, back and forth. "Okay, here's what we do," she announced. "I'll be you again and you be me. Tomorrow I'll get your dad to take me horseback riding, and you get Diane to take you."

"Then what?" Alyssa asked.

Amanda grinned. "Leave the rest to me," she said. "I'm great at this kind of stuff, remember? I have a plan!"

# Chapter 13

The next day Amanda and Alyssa put their plan into action. Amanda and Roger went for a horseback ride in the woods. So did Alyssa and Diane. Then Amanda snuck away from Roger, and Alyssa snuck away from Diane. They hid with their horses behind a tree.

Suddenly, Diane raced by on her horse. Diane wasn't a great rider. In fact, she wasn't even a *good* rider. "Amanda!" she yelled. "Where are you?"

Amanda reached for the slingshot in her pocket. She put a small stone in it and aimed. The stone went flying and hit the horse's rear end. The horse gave a loud whinny and bolted.

"Whoa, horsie! Whoa!" Diane screamed.

A second later, Roger galloped into sight on his horse. He chased after Diane. Amanda and Alyssa held their breath. Roger grabbed Diane's horse and made it stop.

"Thank goodness you came along. You saved my life," Diane told Roger.

Just then, Roger got caught by a large tree branch.

*Crash!* He toppled right off his horse. He landed on the ground and winced in pain.

Alyssa gasped and stepped toward her father. Amanda held her back. "Wait," Amanda whispered. "Diane can take care of this!"

Diane held up two fingers. "How many fingers here, cowboy?" they heard her ask.

Roger sat up and groaned. "Six?"

"Close enough," Diane said. She helped him stand up. "Wait a minute," Diane said. "Are you Roger Callaway—of the Callaway Foundation for Kids?"

"I think so," Roger answered.

"I'm Diane Barrows," Diane told him. "I've always wanted to meet you," Diane said. "The camp's a really big hit with my kids," Diane continued.

"You have kids?" Roger asked.

"No," Diane answered. "I mean, just the kids

from Camp Callaway. I work with them."

She and Roger smiled at each other.

"I was with a camper, but I think she rode back to camp," Diane told Roger.

"I was with my daughter, but I think she rode back to our house," Roger told Diane. "I'd like to hear more about the camp," he added. "Would you like to come over to the house?"

"Sure. If we can walk there," Diane told him. "No more horseback riding for me."

"Okay," Roger agreed.

"Yes!" Amanda cried. She and Alyssa slapped a high-five.

They followed Roger and Diane back to the mansion and hid under a rolling table on the terrace. They had a clear view as Diane placed a bandage over the cut on Roger's forehead. They were getting along great.

"Miss Kensington is calling!" Vincenzo announced. He rushed onto the terrace with the portable telephone. Roger held the receiver to his ear and winced.

"Alyssa did what?" he gasped. "She put bubble gum in your hair?"

Under the cart, Alyssa and Amanda grinned at each other.

"Well, I'm sure it wasn't on purpose," Roger said. "Yes. I'll speak with her," he added.

Diane started to get up. Roger put his hand over the mouthpiece. "Please, I won't be a minute," he told Diane.

"Is there a woman there with you, Roger?" Clarice asked suspiciously.

"Well, sort of...a woman," Roger began. "She's from the camp."

Diane had heard enough. She stood and walked across the yard, heading back to camp.

Alyssa groaned. "They were doing great," she said to Amanda. "What happened?"

Amanda didn't answer. She was too busy working on plan number two.

Alyssa was back at Camp Callaway, pretending to be Amanda. She sat with the other kids around an open campfire. The kids were roasting marshmallows. Alyssa was listening to Diane.

"So this guy comes riding along," Diane was saying. "He saves my life, he's worth a billion dollars, he's totally cute, and to top it all off, he's a really nice guy. And stupid me—I think he likes me," Diane said. "And that he's available."

"He is!" Alyssa blurted out.

"How would you know?" Diane asked.

Alyssa put her hands on her hips. "Was he wearing a wedding ring?" she asked.

"All right smarty-pants. So maybe he's available. That doesn't mean he's interested in me."

"You shouldn't put yourself down," Alyssa told her.

The next evening, Alyssa was on her way to meet Diane at her office before dinner. Suddenly, Alyssa's mouth fell open. Her father was pulling into the driveway in his favorite car!

"It's him!" Alyssa cried. She ran behind Diane's office door to hide. She couldn't let her father find her pretending to be Amanda.

Diane looked up from her desk. "You already saved my life, Mr. Callaway. What can I do for you?"

"I came over to apologize," Roger said. "I was rude to you yesterday. I should never have taken that call. So I'd like to make it up to you. There's a great little pizza joint in town," Roger told her.

Alyssa was so excited. Their plan had worked after all!

Suddenly, a finger tapped Alyssa's shoulder. She nearly screamed out loud.

Frankie stood behind her. "Come on, Amanda," he said. "We're serving tonight."

"Serving what?" Alyssa asked.

"Duh! Dinner!" Frankie replied. "It's our turn to be waiters."

Alyssa raised her eyebrows. Her? Serving food

to other people? She laughed out loud. Not in a
million years!

# Chapter 14

Alyssa lifted the heavy food tray onto her shoulder and sighed. It was fun pretending to be Amanda. Too bad that meant doing Amanda's job too.

The mess hall was filled with noise. The kids were banging their knives and forks again. Alyssa struggled with the heavy tray. She headed toward her table. And stopped. She was in shock.

Roger was sitting at her table with Diane. They hadn't gone out to eat in a restaurant. They were eating here at camp!

Alyssa whirled around and scooted behind the kitchen doors. She peeked outside.

Carmen scooped up her tray and brought it to

Diane and Roger's table.

"Where's Amanda?" Diane asked Carmen.

"I don't know. One minute she's behind me, the next..." Carmen shrugged.

"Well, go find her, okay?" Diane said. "I want her to meet someone."

Carmen ran into the kitchen and grabbed Alyssa. Alyssa grabbed the tall chef's hat right off the cook's head. She crammed it on. It covered her whole face. Carmen dragged her to Diane's table.

Roger laughed when he saw her. "Well, well. My compliments to the chef," he joked.

Carmen tried to pull the hat off Alyssa's head, but Alyssa held on tight. She pulled away.

*I've got to do something*, she thought.

A kid was walking past with a huge bowl of macaroni and cheese. Alyssa stuck out her foot and tripped him.

The kid went sprawling. The bowl went flying. It flew over the table. *Smack!* It hit Roger Callaway right in the face!

Nobody moved. Nobody breathed.

Roger was covered with macaroni and cheese. He reached up and wiped macaroni off his head. He picked up a pat of butter and put it on his spoon. He aimed the spoon at Diane.

"You wouldn't dare," Diane warned him.

*Whap!* The butter hit her on the forehead!

Alyssa peered out from under her chef's hat.

*"Food Fight!"* someone screamed.

Macaroni and cheese sailed over Alyssa's head. She scurried across the floor. She ran through the kitchen and flew out the back door. Amanda was there waiting for her.

"That was great! I couldn't have done it better myself!" Amanda exclaimed.

The girls looked through the mess hall window and saw Diane and Roger huddled together under a table. The food fight raged all around them.

"Look at them," Amanda said.

Suddenly, Alyssa pulled Amanda behind a tree. "Shhhhh! They're coming out!"

Diane and Roger burst out of the mess hall. They walked side by side, laughing happily.

Roger gazed into Diane's eyes. "You're a really special lady," he said.

Diane smiled and slipped her hand into his.

"Wow," Alyssa whispered. "They like each other!"

All of a sudden, Roger took off, running. He was headed right toward the lake.

"What's wrong with him?" Amanda asked.

"Beats me. I've never seen him act like this," Alyssa said, shaking her head.

Amanda and Alyssa followed Roger and Diane

down to the lake. They hid behind a tall wooden rack that held the canoes.

Amanda peeked out. "They're swimming!" she exclaimed.

Alyssa peeked too. Diane and her father were splashing in the water like a couple of campers. Roger leaned close to Diane. Diane leaned close to Roger.

Alyssa held her breath. Were they going to kiss?

Amanda pushed against the canoe rack. She was trying to get a closer look.

*Crash!* The wooden rack crashed to the ground. Amanda and Alyssa went flying.

Diane leapt up. "What was that?" she cried.

"I, uh, I think...that was a sign," Roger said softly.

"What do you mean, a sign?" Diane asked. "Wait, I do know what you mean," Diane continued. "It's about your Miss Kensington, right?"

Roger nodded. "We're getting married next month."

"Of course you are," Diane said. She turned away from Roger and waded ashore.

Alyssa's jaw dropped in dismay. "They were so close!" she wailed.

Amanda sighed. "Grown-ups, they think too much. I give up."

"No, we mustn't," Alyssa said. "Haven't you ever heard that the third time's a charm? We just need another plan!"

# Chapter 15

Amanda and Alyssa sat together. They were each writing notes. Amanda held up her note.

"Okay, listen to this," Amanda said. She read her note out loud:

Dear Roger,
You are so totally fresh. Thinking about you drives me mental. Meet me at the place where we met that time with the horses at seven o'clock tonight.

Love,
Diane

Amanda turned to Alyssa. "How's that?" she

81

asked. "Sound okay?"

"Very romantic," Alyssa told her. "Want to hear mine?"

"Yup," Amanda said.

Alyssa cleared her throat. She began to read:

Dear Diane,

Ever since the first time I saw you I can't stop thinking about you. I must see you tonight at seven.

Yours truly,
Roger Callaway

"Perfect!" Amanda cried. "You give your note to Diane. I'll give mine to Roger. They'll meet each other again tonight and fall in love for sure."

It was a great plan. All they had to do now was wait.

Amanda sneaked into the mansion. She was about to slip the note she wrote to Roger onto a table in the hall. She heard a noise and glanced up. And gasped.

Clarice was there!

"You're back," Amanda said in shock. She

took another look at Clarice and tried to keep from laughing out loud. Clarice's hair was chopped short. Amanda knew it was because of the gum she stuck in her hair.

"What, no big hello?" Clarice asked.

"You're not supposed to be here," Amanda said.

Roger hurried down the stairs. "Why aren't you in New York?" he asked Clarice.

Clarice threw herself into Roger's arms. "I had to come back," she told him. "I couldn't stand to be away from you another minute!"

"You were gone only a day," Roger said, looking confused.

"I know. And I was miserable. I've decided we can't wait a minute longer." Clarice smiled at Roger. "Let's get married tomorrow."

"Tomorrow?" Roger's mouth dropped open.

"Yes. We'll go back to New York right away. We can be married in the church tomorrow. It's all arranged." Clarice turned to Amanda.

"Time to get packed, Alyssa," she said. "We're going to the city."

"Right now? It's too soon!" Amanda said. She hoped there was a way she could still get Roger and Diane together.

Clarice clenched her jaw. She turned to Roger. "May I speak to Alyssa—alone, please?" she asked him sharply.

"Sure," Roger agreed. "I guess I'd better start packing," he said. He went back upstairs.

Clarice whirled on Amanda. "Maybe I didn't make myself clear, Alyssa *darling*. We're going back to the city—now. This little act of yours is getting old. Stop stalling."

"I'm not stalling," Amanda said.

Clarice folded her arms across her chest. "No? Alyssa, by the time I was your age, I'd been through three stepmothers. I know what little girls will do to keep their daddies all to themselves."

"But—"

"Alyssa, don't be rude. I'm talking." Clarice took a deep breath and continued. "You've had Roger all to yourself for nine years. But believe me, those days are all over for you. After tomorrow, *I'm* the woman of the house. And *you* are on your way back to a year-round boarding school—whether you like it or not. Any questions?"

Amanda gulped. "One," she said. "What if I told you I'm not Alyssa? My real name is Amanda Lemmon."

Clarice laughed in her face.

Before Amanda could say another word, Roger and Vincenzo came and carried her out to the waiting car. They were headed to New York City.

And there was absolutely no way Amanda could stop them.

# Chapter 16

Alyssa waited at Camp Callaway. Amanda's plan was sure to work. Any minute now, Diane and Roger would meet again. And her father would never marry Clarice.

"Amanda!" someone called out behind her.

Alyssa turned to see two very weird-looking people hurrying towards her.

"Surprise, Amanda, honey," a very large woman called. "It's us—Fanny and Harry Butkis."

The Butkises! Alyssa gasped. Amanda had told her all about these horrible people!

"Come to Mama, sweetheart!" Fanny Butkis opened her arms and rushed toward Alyssa.

Alyssa took a step away from her.

Harry smiled at Alyssa. "Now, now, don't worry, Amanda. It's all taken care of. Why, the children's shelter said we could get you earlier than we planned."

"Isn't that wonderful?" Fanny Butkis beamed. "You're coming home with us right now, little lady!"

Alyssa took a deep breath. "But...but...I'm not Amanda!" she said.

Fanny and Harry didn't listen. They carried Alyssa to the van that was waiting nearby. The van sped down the driveway.

"Wait!" Alyssa yelled. She glanced out the window. Diane was racing toward the van. Alyssa banged hard on the window. "Diane!" she yelled. "Help!"

"Amanda? Hey! *Hey!*" Diane screamed after the speeding van. "Come back here!"

Alyssa couldn't believe her eyes.

"These are your new brothers and sisters," Mr. Butkis told her.

Alyssa was standing in the Butkis kitchen. Eight kids glared at her. They were all shapes and sizes. But they were all wearing the same dirty blue overalls.

Alyssa took a deep breath. "Look, there's been

a big mistake," she tried to explain. "My name's not Amanda. Really, I'm not—"

"We know that," Mrs. Butkis told her happily. "You don't ever have to be Amanda again."

"That's right," Mr. Butkis agreed. "From now on you're little Betty Butkis." He turned to the Butkis children. "Kids, scoot over. Give Betty here some cereal."

Mrs. Butkis smiled. "And after breakfast, you'll get to see where Daddy works. Won't that be fun?"

Alyssa swallowed. It didn't sound like any fun at all.

Alyssa soon found out that the Butkis kids had to work. And work *hard*. The Butkises owned a scrap metal yard. It was a dirty, grimy place piled high with old hunks of tin and steel. The kids had to clean it up.

As soon as Alyssa could sneak away for a few minutes, she found a telephone. She called the lake house, but no one answered.

*I'll try the apartment in New York*, Alyssa decided. She dialed quickly. Amanda answered the phone.

"Amanda, you've got to help me," Alyssa said. "I'm at the Butkises. These people are scary. You've got to get me out of here. And fast!"

"Okay, but I've got news for you," Amanda told her. "Your dad's getting married. In exactly two hours and twelve minutes."

"Oh, no!" Alyssa cried. "What do we do now?"

"I don't know," Amanda told her. "But it had better be good."

Amanda burst into Vincenzo's room. She found him dressed up in his fancy suit for the wedding. Amanda was also dressed for the wedding. She wore a beautiful flower girl dress.

"Vinnie! They took Alyssa away!" she cried. "I'm not the real Alyssa," she explained. "You've got to believe me! I'm Amanda. Amanda Lemmon!"

Vincenzo gazed calmly at her. "Please, Alyssa. Don't start this again. You tried that all the way into the city."

"I can prove I'm not Alyssa," Amanda said. "You've taken care of Alyssa all her life, right?" Amanda said.

"Alyssa, not this again," Vincenzo said, annoyed.

"Answer the question," Amanda said.

"Right," Vincenzo agreed.

"So you know everything about her. Every bruise, every freckle, every scar. Right?"

"You could say that," Vincenzo replied.

Amanda showed him a deep scar on her leg. "I got that playing baseball. Do you remember it?"

Vincenzo frowned. "No, I don't," he admitted. "But that doesn't prove a thing."

"Then why don't you tell me how I got this scar?" Amanda pulled back her hair. She leaned close to Vincenzo.

Vincenzo stared at the jagged scar on her forehead. He had never seen it before. His eyes widened in shock.

"You're not Alyssa!" he cried.

"Nope. Name's Amanda," Amanda told him.

"Wait," Vincenzo said. "If you're here, then Alyssa is…"

"In a whole lot of trouble," Amanda finished.

Vincenzo headed for the door. "I've got to tell Mr. Callaway."

"Wait!" Amanda stopped him. "We've got to get him to see Diane one more time before the wedding. Please don't tell him. Not yet. It will work. They'll fall in love, and Clarice will be history."

Amanda held her breath. Would Vincenzo help her?

Vincenzo narrowed his eyes. He stared at Amanda. "Okay," he finally said. "I'll help you. But I hope you have a plan."

# Chapter 17

Amanda hid behind a door in the children's shelter. Vincenzo and Diane were in Amanda's old room. They were arguing. Amanda strained to hear what they were saying.

Vincenzo's voice rose. "Listen carefully," he told Diane. "I'm here for Alyssa Callaway. You have her, and I want her back."

"What are you talking about?" Diane stared at him. "I don't have Alyssa Callaway. I have never even met Alyssa Callaway."

"Oh, but you have." Vincenzo showed Diane a photograph. "*This* is Alyssa Callaway."

Diane glanced at the photo. She stared at Vincenzo. "Look, Vinnie. Maybe you should get your eyes checked. This little girl's name is Amanda Lemmon."

"No," Vincenzo told her calmly. He handed Diane a different photograph. It showed Amanda dressed in her party outfit, sitting at the piano at Roger's engagement party.

Diane stared at both of the photos.

"There are two of them," she said. "And they look exactly alike!"

"Right," Vincenzo told her. "My Alyssa looks like your Amanda. But you have Alyssa—and you must return her to me immediately. If you do, I'll see that you aren't punished."

Diane gaped at him. "But...I don't have her," she tried to explain. "She was adopted by— uh—the Butkis family."

"Then I suggest you un-adopt her," Vincenzo said. "And quickly. Mr. Callaway is getting married in ninety minutes. Alyssa must be at the wedding."

Diane gasped. "I can't bring your Alyssa back that fast."

Vincenzo wrote down a phone number on a piece of paper and handed it to Diane. "You can if you call this number. My friend will help you. But remember—be at St. Bart's Church in ninety minutes."

Diane gazed at him in dismay. "I'll do my

best," she said. "Right away."

Amanda raced down the stairs. She beat Vincenzo back to the car. "So?" she asked. "Will she do it?"

"I believe so," Vincenzo answered.

"Vinnie, my man!" Amanda yelled. She slapped him a high-five.

It was a beautiful day for a wedding. St. Bart's Church was packed with guests. The women wore long, flowing gowns, and the men wore crisp new tuxedos. Amanda and Vincenzo waited nervously on the steps of the church.

"What's taking them so long?" Amanda was worried. "Are you sure you told Diane the right place?"

"Yes," Vincenzo answered. "I told her St. Bart's Church." He peered down the street.

Amanda pulled at the collar of her flower girl dress. She made a face. "How can you be so calm at a time like this?"

"They'll be here," Vincenzo said.

Amanda cracked her knuckles. "I hope so. We just have to stop this wedding!"

Amanda thought about Alyssa. She spent a whole night at the Butkises. Amanda shuddered. But if their plan could stop Roger from marrying Clarice, it would be worth it!

Inside, the last of the wedding guests were seated. Amanda and Vincenzo were called inside. The wedding was about to start.

Music filled the church. "Where's the flower girl?" a nervous man asked.

Amanda raised her hand. "That's me," she said.

The man handed Amanda a basket of flower petals. "There we go. Remember, it's—"

Amanda rolled her eyes. "Step, petal, drop. I know! I know!"

She glanced at the church doors one last time.

*Still no sign of Diane and Alyssa,* she thought.

The nervous man pushed Amanda into the aisle. "Go," he whispered loudly. He gave Amanda a push.

The crowd of people in the church turned to gaze at her. Amanda waved at all of them.

"Hi, how ya doing, everyone? Thanks for coming to the wedding!"

Clarice stuck her head into the church aisle. "Get moving!" she whispered harshly.

*I can't stall 'em too much longer,* Amanda thought.

She began taking tiny steps down the aisle. She glanced nervously back toward the doors. *Where are they?!*

"Enough of this!" Clarice shouted. She lifted

up the skirt of her long wedding gown and raced down the aisle.

"All right, I'm here," Clarice yelled. "Let's get married. Right now!"

*Uh-oh,* thought Amanda. *Now what do I do?*

# Chapter 18

Alyssa couldn't believe how mean the Butkises were. And their kids were mean too.

"Here, your majesty," Brenda Butkis said in a nasty voice. "We brought you something." Brenda handed Alyssa a crown made out of a rusty tin can. "Put it on," Brenda told her.

Alyssa fought back tears. The Butkis kids also made her wear an old greasy blanket. They said it was a queen's robe.

"You keep telling us that you're really a rich kid," Bobby Butkis said. "Well, this stuff will make you feel like the Queen of the Scrap Yard."

"My name is Alyssa Callaway!" Alyssa screamed at them.

"Prove it," Bobby Butkis answered.

At that moment a loud roar filled the sky.

Alyssa glanced up. So did all the Butkises.

A huge helicoper flew overhead. It landed in the middle of the scrap metal yard. The Butkises ran away from it.

The door of the helicopter opened, and Diane jumped out.

"Come on, Alyssa!" Diane cried. "We have to get you to a wedding!"

Alyssa threw down the crown and the dirty blanket. She turned to the Butkises. "Told you I was Alyssa," she said.

Mr. Butkis tried to stop Alyssa from leaving. "You're my kid now," he told her.

"Get out of our way," Diane growled. "Or else!"

Mr. Butkis backed away from Diane. "Okay— take her," he said.

*Yes!* Alyssa cheered silently.

Diane and Alyssa flew into New York City. The helicopter landed in the middle of Central Park. Alyssa and Diane jumped out. "Thanks," Diane told the helicopter driver.

"Thank Vincenzo," he answered. "He set this up."

Diane grabbed Alyssa's hand. "Now we need a taxi," Diane told her.

But there were no taxicabs in sight.

A horse and carriage stood in the park. The driver was not in the carriage. He was buying himself a hot dog from a nearby hot dog stand.

"Diane, come on," Alyssa shouted.

Alyssa climbed up into the driver's seat of the carriage. She grabbed the horse's reins.

Diane hollered to the driver. "This is an emergency! Thanks for your help."

"Heeyaa!" Alyssa yelled at the horse. And the carriage took off.

Amanda watched helplessly. Inside the church, the wedding finally began.

Roger and Clarice stood together in front of all the guests. Roger looked uncomfortable. He stared at Clarice. "I—I can't marry you," he said.

The guests gasped out loud.

Clarice was stunned. "What did you say?" she asked.

"I'm sorry, Clarice," Roger told her. "I can't marry you. I'm in love with someone else."

"You…you…" Clarice sputtered.

"Wait!" someone cried.

Amanda whirled. It was Alyssa and Diane!

They hurried toward the front of the church.

"All right!" Amanda cheered.

There was a stunned silence. Everyone stared

at the two girls who looked exactly alike.

Roger gaped from one Alyssa to the other.

Clarice's mouth dropped open. "Eaaaah!" she shrieked in horror. "There are *two* of them!"

Clarice glared at Alyssa, who was closest to her. "This is all your fault!" she screamed. "Why don't you go back where you belong?"

Diane stepped within an inch of Clarice's face. "Back off, bozo," she warned her.

Clarice's mouth dropped open in shock. "You *all* ruined my wedding," she shouted. "I've never been so embarrassed in my life!"

Clarice whirled around, getting ready to storm out of the church. Alyssa lifted her foot. She stomped down hard on the back of Clarice's long dress.

There was a loud tearing sound. The back of the dress ripped off. Alyssa, Amanda, Roger, and Diane burst out laughing. Clarice ran out of the church with her underwear showing.

"It's about time you showed up!" Amanda told Alyssa.

"We got here as soon as we could," Alyssa explained.

Amanda and Alyssa hugged each other. Roger gaped at the two girls. He blinked in confusion.

"But this is impossible," he said.

"Nothing's impossible," Amanda told Roger.

"Right, Alyssa?" Amanda nudged Alyssa in the ribs. They grinned at each other.

Amanda held out a hand to Roger. "My real name's Amanda," she said. She jerked her thumb toward Diane. "I'm with her."

Roger gazed happily at Diane. "You just saved my life."

"I'm sorry I broke up your party. But I didn't want the wrong girl going down the aisle. I mean, the wrong flower girl," Diane said.

Roger smiled. "I think you had it right the first time."

Alyssa grinned at Amanda. "I told you we could do it," she said. "Third time's a charm."

Alyssa and Amanda both turned to Roger and Diane. "So, kiss already!" they said at the same time.

Roger took Diane in his arms. He gave her a long, romantic kiss.

Alyssa and Amanda slapped a high-five. Diane and Roger studied the two girls.

"They're awfully cute together," Diane told Roger.

"I can't tell which one is Alyssa and which is Amanda," Roger told Diane. "I guess we'll have to keep both of them."

Amanda held her breath. Alyssa held *her* breath.

Diane raised an eyebrow. "We?" she asked.

"That's right," Roger answered. "We'll be one big, happy family."

All right! Roger and Diane were getting married.

Amanda and Alyssa held out their hands for another high-five.

"Put 'er there..." Amanda began.

"...sister!" Alyssa finished for her.

# COMING IN APRIL!

# The Adventures of MARY-KATE & ASHLEY™

A brand new book series starring the Olsen Twins!
Based on their best-selling detective
home video series.

Join the Trenchcoat Twins™—Mary-Kate and
Ashley—as they find mystery, adventure and fun!

**Book One:**
*The Case of the Sea World Adventure*
**Book Two:**
*The Case of the Mystery Cruise*

**Look for these great books this April and
all year long from *Scholastic*.**

It doesn't matter if you live around the corner...
or around the world...
If you are a fan of Mary-Kate and Ashley Olsen,
you should be a member of

# MARY-KATE + ASHLEY'S FUN CLUB™

Here's what you get:
**Our Funzine™**
An autographed color photo
Two black & white individual photos
A full size color poster
An official **Fun Club™** membership card
A **Fun Club™** school folder
Two special **Fun Club™** surprises
Birthday & holiday cards
**Fun Club™** collectibles catalog
Plus a **Fun Club™** box to keep everything in

To join Mary-Kate + Ashley's Fun Club™, fill out the form
below and send it along with $17.00 ($22.00 for Canadian,
$27.00 for International - **U.S. FUNDS ONLY PLEASE!**) to:

## MARY-KATE + ASHLEY'S FUN CLUB™
## 859 HOLLYWOOD WAY, SUITE 275
## BURBANK, CA 91505

NAME:_____

ADDRESS:_____

CITY:_____ STATE:_____ ZIP:_____

PHONE: (____)_____ BIRTHDATE:_____

If membership is shared by two or more children please include all
birthdates and $2.00 per child to cover postage and handling for
additional birthday and holiday cards.
NOTE: ADDITIONAL CHILDREN MUST LIVE IN SAME HOUSEHOLD.

# The Adventures of MARY-KATE & ASHLEY™

**Look for these best-selling detective home video episodes!**
**Starring the Trenchcoat Twins™—your favorite stars**
**Mary-Kate & Ashley Olsen!**

---

---

DUALSTAR VIDEO

Distributed by KidVision, a division of WARNERVISION ENTERTAINMENT.

TM & © 1995 Dualstar Entertainment Group. Inc.